John Madison Morton

My First Fit of the Gout

An Original Farce in One Act

John Madison Morton

My First Fit of the Gout
An Original Farce in One Act

ISBN/EAN: 9783743666832

Printed in Europe, USA, Canada, Australia, Japan

Cover: Foto ©Andreas Hilbeck / pixelio.de

More available books at **www.hansebooks.com**

MY FIRST FIT OF THE GOUT.

AN ORIGINAL FARCE,

IN ONE ACT.

BY

JOHN MADDISON MORTON,

AUTHOR OF

*" Box and Cox," " A Desperate Game," " To Paris and Back
for Five Pounds," " Two Bonnycastles," " My Precious
Betsy," " Going to the Derby,"
&c., &c., &c.*

THOMAS HAILES LACY,

WELLINGTON STREET, STRAND,

LONDON.

First Performed at the Queen's Theatre,
March, 1835.

CHARACTERS.

SIR GEORGE MARTYR	. . .	Mr. WRENCH.
CAPTAIN ARUNDEL	. . .	Mr.
TONY	. . . . .	Mr. MORRIS BARNETT.
LADY JANET	. . . .	Miss JANE MORDAUNT.
BELINDA	. . . .	Mrs. NISBETT.
SERVANT GIRLS, &c.		

SCENE—LONDON.

COSTUMES OF THE DAY.

Time in Representation, Fifty-five Minutes.

MY FIRST FIT OF THE GOUT.

SCENE.—*A modern handsomely-furnished Apartment—Table, sofa, large arm-chair, &c. &c.—Doors* R. *and* L., *and folding-doors in* C.

LADY JANET *and* BELINDA *discovered, seated.*

LADY J. (*rising*) Nay, but, my dear Belinda——

BEL. (*rising*) Nay, but, my dear Lady Janet, you shall not submit to it. What! allow that rakish husband of yours to play the gallant under your own pretty nose? *I* won't bear it, if *you* will. But perhaps you don't love the fellow?

LADY J. Ah—too dearly!

BEL. The truth is, Nature has given him handsome legs, but a very shabby understanding. *Love* has nothing to do with *his* vagaries,—'tis *vanity*, of which he has more than would supply a regiment of our sex, though they all were *blues*. I would make his head heavier than his heels, if he were my husband.

LADY J. You really surprise me, and know more of my husband's frailties than I do.

BEL. Simply because he makes more love to me than he does to you.

LADY J. (*shocked*) Belinda!

BEL. (*imitating her tone of surprise*) Belinda!

LADY J. Love to you? Impossible!

BEL. Come, that's complimentary, at all events.

LADY J. Nay, while I do justice to his taste, I must feel my wrongs.

BEL. Wrongs? That is too harsh a word for such follies. Were it love, would I encourage him as I do?

LADY J. You encourage him, girl?

BEL. (*imitating*) You encourage him, girl? To be sure. Is it not better that he should devote his attentions to one whose pleasure it will be to torment *him*, than to one whose pleasure it would be to torment *you*? Besides, have I not another reason for bringing to shame and contrition this husband of yours, and this guardian of mine?—for, while he holds the control of my fortune, poor Captain Arundel, whose life, I believe, depends on my smiles——

LADY J. Now I understand. You benevolently undertake the Herculean task of reforming the husband, solely to promote the

wife's happiness, and save to his country the life of its nursling
Hannibal, Captain Arundel.

BEL. Exactly.

LADY J. How disinterested—how noble!

BEL. Ain't it? But how shall we plague this husband?

LADY J. My study has been to *please* him.

BEL. And that's the reason he *plagues* you. Dear, dear—here
are two women who cannot contrive a bit of mischief! Why, we
are a disgrace to our sex! I have it,—make him jealous!

LADY J. No,—I will not excite attention in his eyes by making
myself despicable in my own.

BELL *rings*.

—There's his bell. Where can his man Tony be? Why does he
keep that dolt?

BEL. Because he *is* a dolt, and don't pry into his master's secrets.

BELL *rings again violently*.

Enter TONY R.H., *carrying a pair of boots, and peeping into a*
letter.

LADY J. So it seems. (*tapping* TONY *on the shoulder*) What are
you peeping at?

TONY. Oh! I was only looking at that picture through this. All
your virtuosises look at pictures through a hole.

BEL. Indeed! (*looking through the letter*) It certainly does give
an insight into many concealed beauties. (*reads—aside*) "Do not
fail,"—"masquerade." Signed "Somebody." (*returns letter to*
TONY)

LADY J. Tony, don't you hear Sir George's bell?

TONY. In course.

LADY J. Then ought you not to run?

TONY. Oh, in course I ought; but——

BEL. (*sharply*) But what?

TONY. Don't frown, Miss, or I shall expire. May I tell your
Ladyships my story? You must know I'm a great story-teller.

LADY J. Probably.

BELL *rings*.

—But Sir George is ringing again.

TONY. In course—he likes it, or he wouldn't do it. Ah! he little
knows——

BEL. What?

TONY. That I'm in love! If he did, he would not be in such a
tough passion, and pay so little respect to my tender one, and wouldn't
use his handsome foot in a manner it would be a breach of good man-
ners to mention.

BEL. In love, Tony? And who is the envied object of your
adoration?

TONY. Who? Oh! (*sighs*) That's part of my story.

BEL. Well, let's have it.

TONY. Well, and so, you must know, the fire that consumes me
began last frost. I had been sitting on the coach-box, at *Almanacks*,

till I was an icicle; and so, you must know, a certain lady—oh dear!
—(*looks at* BELINDA)—in stepping into the coach, slipped, and fell
into my arms. My heart melted like a lump of ice in the dog-days.
Don't you remember it, Miss?

BEL. *I* remember? Heavens! am *I*——

TONY. Yes! Now the murder's out!

BEL. Tony, you are mad!

TONY. Oh! in course, I'm getting into the lunatic line. Don't
smile, Miss—that makes me worse. I've kept the step of the coach
soaped ever since, in the hope of another slip.

LADY J. What can be done with the fool?

TONY. That's what I want to know. I've been to the doctor's
about it.

BEL. The doctor's?—about me?

'TONY. No—about *me*. He cured one of the coach-horses of the
staggers, so I thought he might give me something for my poor,
palpitating heart.

LADY J. But what has your stupid, palpitating heart to do with
your master's boots?

TONY. That's what I'm coming to in my story. Well, and so, you
must know, as I was a fetching master's new boots home just now,
from the bootmaker's, I thought I'd call on the doctor about my
" stupid, palpitating heart," as you call it. So I did, and the doctor
laughed at me, and said I had got the rheumatics, and gave me
some *embarkation* to rub myself with.

BEL. An embarkation?

TONY. Yes—a notion.

BEL. A lotion, stupid!

TONY. Well, he said it would smart pretty tightish at first, but
that I wasn't to mind that. Well, and so, you must know, as I was
sauntering home from the doctor's—in course not thinking what I
was about—a cab upset me into the kennel, and decanted the inflam-
matory fluid into this boot. Now, if master was to put it on, he'd
be tickled in fine style.

BEL. (*apart to* LADY JANET) My dear friend—the happiest
thought! I'll make *my* lover what few lovers are—useful as well as
ornamental. Look at him. Ha, ha, ha! Ought not I to be flattered? (*aloud*) Tony, I'm going to confide in your honour——

TONY. Don't too far, for fear——

BEL. And to trust you with a secret. Lady Janet is jealous of
her husband.

TONY. Jealous, is she? *Rub* her!

BEL. (*concealing a laugh*) Rub her! Had we not better rub her
husband, who makes her so?

TONY. In course,—but how?

BEL. Let him wear these boots; and when he feels the tickling
sensations you speak of, you can hint 'tis what he most dreads.

TONY. I know—his first fit of the gout!

BEL. Now, take the boots to your master.

TONY. Yes; but I'd better drop a little more of the *embarkation*
into 'em first, just to make sure. And must we part?

BEL. Prudence requires it. We must be secret.

TONY. In course we must.

BEL. You'll be faithful, Tony?

TONY. Till death!

Exit, sighing, R.H.

BEL. Ha, ha, ha! Yes, yes—I see it all.

LADY J. What?—where?

BEL. "In my mind's eye, Horatio." If the boot does its duty, I'll answer for the cure.

LADY J. How?

BEL. By humbling his vanity, till he is as miserable as any amiable woman could wish her husband to be.

LADY J. But I don't want to torment him.

BEL. Not torment your husband? Indeed, my dear, you have very confined notions of matrimonial gratifications. But never mind; you may administer the sweets—I'll provide the bitters. Can you affect indifference to his gallantries?

LADY J. I'll try.

BEL. Can you laugh at his fears of the gout?

LADY J. Heartily.

BEL. Can you keep him at home till the foot begins to twinge?

LADY J. I don't know how.

BEL. I do. Ask him to go out with you.

LADY J. (*offended*) 'Tis possible he might find my companionship not so disagreeable.

BEL. Oh, oh! I'm glad I have roused your Ladyship's vanity.

LADY J. But should he condescend to walk with his wife?

BEL. Then—oh! then say you expect *me* here, and he will be as fixed in his chair in Belgrave Square as King Charles in his saddle at Charing Cross.

LADY J. The vanity of some ladies requires no exciting.

BEL. Do not shake those pretty locks at me, but trust to my generalship.

SIR GEORGE *heard without, calling* "Tony!"

—Here comes Sir George. Now for operations. Don't pout, and her hubby sha'n't look at any pretty face but her own! There—come along!

Exeunt, BELINDA *bantering*, R.

Enter SIR GEORGE, *in dressing-gown and slippers*, L.

SIR G. Tony, Tony! I wish the stupid fellow would come with my boots. I'm very particular about my boots, because constriction of the ankle sometimes produces enlargement, which, egad! might end in the gout,—horrible idea! How stand my interesting engagements? (*seats himself, and takes out a memorandum book*) The divine Belinda promised to call at one. Rosamond's box at the Opera to be engaged,—the poor thing thinks it wrong to prefer me; but if she can't help it, what's to be done? The mask and domino of the fair incognita, who corresponds under the soubriquet of

"Somebody," to be selected. Now some people might, from these little gallantries, imagine that I was indifferent to my wife,—on the contrary, I adore her! And what father delights more in his children than I do?—or feels more paternal joy when he hears their carolling shouts—at an agreeable distance? (*locks a door*) Why, Tony! How that booby loiters! 'Tis certainly convenient to have an unsuspecting simpleton about you, but one may have too much of a good thing.

Enter TONY *with boots*, R.H.

—You've got the boots?

TONY. In course I have.

SIR G. (*taking one*) That's right.

TONY. No—that's left.

SIR G. Ha, ha! Tony, you're an ass!

TONY. Oh, that, in course, Sir.

SIR G. (*pulling on boots*) They don't pinch much.

TONY. Don't they?

SIR G. They'll be quite easy—*by-and-bye*.

TONY. (*aside*) Will they?

SIR G. (*admiring his foot*) Tony, that's what I call a fit!

TONY. A fit! What, already?

SIR G. What do you mean by already?

TONY. I thought you meant a fit of the gout.

SIR G. The gout! Hark'ee! never dare to breathe that atrocious monosyllable in my presence—you know 'tis what I dread. The very idea has made me feel as if 'twere coming.

TONY. Indeed! (*aside*) Then 'tis time I was going. (*aloud*) Here's a letter—(*trying to make it flat*)—from Somebody.

SIR G. (*alarmed*) Who told you, Sir, that it came from Somebody?

TONY. Nobody—but in course somebody wrote it.

SIR G. (*smiling*) True! Where's my wife?

TONY. With Miss Belinda. (*sighs*)

SIR G. (*affectedly*) Belinda's a fine creature! I think, Tony, you're a bit of a favourite.

TONY. (*looking at himself complacently*) Why, I rather flatter myself——

SIR G. Well, 'pon my life, that's exceedingly comic! By-the-bye, to-day I run a match with her supposed lover, Captain Arundel. I shall beat him!

TONY. Beat him! (*aside*) Damn him!—murder him!

SIR G. And shall give him the go-by as easily as in the race where Cupid holds the garland of victory, which the Graces weave.

TONY. (*imitating* SIR GEORGE) Well, upon my life, that's exceeding comic!

SIR G. Comic! Get out, you impertinent——

TONY. (*is moving off*)

SIR G. (*in a loud voice calls him back*) Tony!

TONY. (*starting*) Sir!

SIR G. Come here, Sir—nearer.

TONY. Yes, Sir!

SIR G. This boot——

Tony. (*starting back*) Eh?

Sir G. This boot feels very strange.

Tony. In course it does—'tis a new one.

Sir G. And damp!

Tony. (*retreating by degrees*) Damp!—you only fancy it, Sir.

Sir G. I don't fancy it at all, Sir! Abscond!

Tony. In course, Sir. (*meeting* Lady Janet, *points to* Sir George) The boot is on—and I'm off!

> *Exit, mimicking the pains of the gout,* R.

Lady J. Dear Sir George!

Sir G. (*rises to meet her*) My sweet Janet! (*kisses her*) Going out, love?

Lady J. Yes, with you, if you please.

Sir G. (*aside*) That's a poser!

Lady J. (*aside*) Belinda was right. (*aloud*) So go and dress, dear, (*takes his arm*) and—we'll take *all* the children with us.

Sir G. My dear Janet, nothing would delight me more than to take a walk with you and *all* the children; but you know what I dread; and I feel a sort of gouty twinging in this foot that really alarms me.

Lady J. Then, deary, I'll send for the darlings, and we'll keep you company the whole of the day.

Sir G. Delightful thought! (*aside*) What a bore! (*aloud*) But shall my happiness be purchased at the cost of your health, and that of the darling babes? You are pale, my love—you are indeed ; and when you know I adore the bloom that exercise gives, you will walk for my gratification, and take *all* the children with you ;—besides, (*in an endearing tone*) you walk so elegantly—you do indeed! (*aside*) She smiles—she takes the bait !

Lady J. (*aside*) He flatters himself he has done it cleverly. (*aloud*) Then you insist?

Sir G. When your health is in question, I own myself a bashaw! I *do* insist.

Lady J. Well, then, by-bye! I'll *soon be back.*

Sir G. (*endearingly*) I had rather you took your time,—walking too quickly might distress the dear children.

> *Exit* Lady Janet R.

Sir G. (*looking after her*) Sweet, confiding creature! How delightful to have such a companion! I thought she never would have gone! Egad, I'm an enviable fellow! A noble fortune—a wife who does me honour—a tailor who does me justice—and a shoemaker, I flatter myself, *I* do justice to. 'Faith, I must practise that movement in the Mazourka. (*preparing as if to dance*) Ha, ha! (*in an exceedingly serious tone repeats*) Ha, ha! What's that ? A pain,—sudden—strange! Pooh, pooh! alarmed at a twinge?

Enter Belinda R.

Bel. Fie, Sir George! 'Tis not gallant to practise a *pas-seul,* when you might gratify a lady by a *pas-de-deux.*

SIR G. I've got rid of Lady Janet, you little rogue!

BEL. I know,—by pretending to have the gout. Making up an ugly face at your wife was capital acting.

SIR G. (*feeling a twinge, winces*)

BEL. But you need not make an ugly face at *me*, for mocking is catching sometimes. Why, what *is* the matter?

SIR G. (*wincing*) Nothing worth mentioning!

BEL. What! not a smile to thank me for this *tête-à-tête?*

SIR G. (*attempts to smile*)

BEL. Do you call *that* a smile? I never saw such a one, except from a laughing hyæna. But never mind;—here's a guitar, now, for our practice. Come, Sir George.

A PAS-DE-DEUX, *during which, and the preliminary attitudes,* SIR GEORGE *feels severe twinges.*

BEL. Why, Sir George, you are standing on one foot, like a goose going to roost.

SIR G. Am I? Oh! dear—yes—no. (*aside*) I'm annihilated! The gout!—can it be? It is—it must be! Oh! (*falls into a chair*) Come hither, Belinda.

BEL. No, my naughty Guardian, you want to coax me to sit on your knee!

SIR G. (*earnestly*) No, upon my soul, I don't!

Enter TONY R.

TONY. (*looking sulkily, and saying gruffly*) Captain Arundel!

BEL. Show him in.

SIR G. No, no!

TONY. He wants to know if you are ready to run your match.

SIR G. Not quite ready. Go to him, Belinda, and say I've got a fit——

BEL. A fit? You alarm me!

SIR G. Of *laziness*—that's all! Ha, ha, ha! (*changes his tone*) Ho, ho!

BEL. What! send me to entertain your rival?

SIR G. For once, you may have pity on your poor lover.

BEL. Well, then, for once I *have* pity on my poor lover! ha, ha, ha! (*aside*) Tony, is all right?

TONY. His foot's on fire—like my bosom!

Exit BELINDA R.—TONY *looks languishingly after her.*

SIR G. The gout! 'Tis in my brain! I'm delirious! Ha, ha! Tony! See, my tombstone—Sir George Martyr, died of gout, aged thirty-six!

TONY. Nonsense!—you're worth two dead ones.

SIR G. Here am I left alone to perish,—my wife gadding about the town. (*in a voice of thunder*) Tony!

TONY. (*very softly*) Did you call, Sir?

SIR G. No, Sir, I did not call, but I roared, Sir! Look at me, Tony—don't be afraid!

TONY. Afraid? I haven't afraid to look at Old Nick himself!

SIR G. Tony, do you think you could get that boot off if you were to try?

TONY. In course I could. Here goes! (*seizes hold of the boot, and draws it off violently*)

SIR G. Lacerating savage! (*plaintively*) How many of my toes have you got in the boot?

TONY. I'll see, Sir. (*feeling in the boot*)

SIR G. Now, Tony, look at my foot, and on your oath tell me what it is like!

TONY. Why, Sir, it's very like the other one.

SIR G. No more than a constable's staff is like the Monument! Lift it softly on that stool. Gently, you villain!

TONY. Lord, Sir! He, he, he!

SIR G. Don't grin at me!

TONY. Then don't you grin at me, if you come to that.

SIR G. Get out of my sight! Stay—come back! In case of another paroxysm, move all the glass and china out of my way—unload my pistols—draw my razors across the fender; and Tony, I suppose you must get me a pair—of—damn the word, it chokes me!

TONY. Oh, crutches!

SIR G. Yes—I believe that is what they call them; and Tony, tell the servants to keep quiet, as they value my life.

TONY. They won't mind that a bit. I'll tell them to be quiet, as they value their places.

SIR G. And, above all, not to bang the doors.

TONY. In course not.

Exit, slamming the door, R.

SIR G. Savage! The gout—horrible, damnable! The rheumatism I could walk off. If I were bilious, I could send for a Cheltenham horse that understands the *liver trot.* I would not mind the measles, or the mumps. But the gout! I feel I'm altering very fast! My forehead is cracking into wrinkles—my mouth getting lower than my chin! I wonder I'm alive!—I don't believe I am! (*a loud knocking*) Yes, I am, for every noise sends a dagger through me!

Re-enter TONY R.

—Tony, tie a yard of flannel round that infernal knocker!

TONY. Why, the knocker ain't got the gout! He, he, he! (*with emphasis*) Here's *somebody* wants you.

SIR G. *Somebody,* is it? But *nobody* in his senses would permit *Somebody* to walk in.

TONY. In course not. But *somebody* walked in without a permit, and is now talking to Lady Janet.

SIR G. Talking to Lady Janet? I'm very ill!

TONY. My lady's just come home, looking so salutary.

SIR G. Ah! What would I not give now to walk with that dear angel and *all* the children!

TONY. Oh! and please, Sir, the porter has given my lady half-a-dozen *Billy Duxes* for you,—such beauties!

SIR G. Essence of gout! Disgrace and misery! Hark! I hear
them coming! (*nearly crying*) Tony, Tony, what shall I do?

TONY. Put your best leg foremost, and be off!

SIR G. But what is the use of my best leg, if my worst won't
follow? No, that won't do! Run away with me, that's a good
fellow! Open those folding-doors.

TONY. (*opens doors O.*)

SIR G. Suppose this a railroad,—on with your steam! Oh for a
twenty-horse power!

TONY. (*wheels him off rapidly*)

SIR G. (*without*) Mind the stairs, you rascal! (*a loud crash,
and folding-doors are closed again*)

Enter LADY JANET, BELINDA, *and* CAPTAIN ARUNDEL, R.

BEL. A clear stage and good manœuvring ground—eh, Captain?

LADY J. (*displaying billets-doux*) Look here,—*billets-doux*, in
every variety of form and hue.

BEL. Except a *blush* colour! Now, can you, after this, scruple
to punish him?

LADY J. My feelings revolt at your plan; and, but that it may
accomplish your union with Captain Arundel, 1 would not listen to it.

CAPT. A. (*bows*)

BEL. Nor would I, dear coz, if it were not to secure your domestic
happiness. You perceive, Captain, we have no selfish feelings.

CAPT. A. Nor have I. I believe we are all equally disinterested.
Ahem!

BEL. (*to* CAPTAIN ARUNDEL) Now, you must see Sir George,—
talk of me with indifference, (*archly*) if you can,—speak of Lady
Janet in raptures!

CAPT. A. (*gallantly*) Such charms——

BEL. (*stopping his mouth*) We don't want your raptures here.
You are very anxious to begin. March, Sir! And remember, that
though, in your match with Sir George, you may walk over the
course, you'll find the matrimonial one requires you to be warranted
free from vice or blemish.

CAPT. A. (*kisses her hand*)

Exit L.H.

BEL. And now, dearest coz, you, all gaiety and indifference, will
present these variegated *billets-doux* to your husband—while I, with
an onion in my handkerchief, will weep over his woes. Ha, ha, ha!
Come—no pouting. Half-an-hour's levity in the wife, and half-an-
hour's mortification in the husband, will, to all your days and nights
to come, bring what Lady Macbeth says——

LADY J. Heigho!

BEL. "Only look up clear,—
To alter favour ever is to fear,—
Leave all the rest to me."

—As we are all going to act a past, there's a bit of tragedy to begin
with.

Exeunt L.H.

The folding doors are again opened, and SIR GEORGE *is seen seated in the arm-chair—wheels himself forward, after looking about him,—*

SIR G. Oh! such twitchings, and gnawings, and grindings, and crashings—and to be left alone!—to die for what any one cares; no comfort, no support, everybody out,—even my crutches not come home! (*opens secretary-drawer, and takes out jewellery—sighs*) And these bijoux, that I had promised to distribute among the dear girls! Heigho! I'll try and read the paper. This double sheet feels like a wet blanket, and is about as large. "Hasty Sketch of Debates." Nineteen columns,—pleasant! "List of Majority," "Want Places," "Almacks." Ah! now for it! "At this concentration of beauty and rank, Sir George Martyr was the glass of fashion and the mould of form——" Come, that's justice!—I was always an advocate for the liberty of the Press. "His classic tread in the dance is entirely attributed to the matchless blacking sold in bottles——" Pshaw! *runs his fist through the paper*)

Enter TONY, *running, with the crutches,* R.H.

TONY. Here they be, Sir—a pair of nice ones, and I heartily wish you health to wear them. Come, do try to stump about a bit.

SIR G. That ever Sir George Martyr should be asked to stump about a bit! Zounds! here's the Captain! Give me the paper to cover my legs, and hide those infernal crutches! (*places the paper over his knees, while* TONY *places the crutches under the table*)

Enter CAPTAIN ARUNDEL, L.H.

CAPT. A. Why, Sir George, what the deuce ails you, man?

SIR G. Out of condition—lazy! I sha'n't run our match,—there's an I.O.U. for forfeit.

CAPT. A. Thank you! I'll trouble you for a peep at the paper.

SIR G. There is not a word in it, as you may see. I say, Captain, —(*winking at* TONY)—how goes your match with Belinda?

CAPT. A. I'faith I cannot boast of the pace—I begin to think I have a rival.

TONY. (*who has been surveying him with sulky glances, says conceitedly*) I should not wonder!

SIR G. (*aside to* TONY) He has found that out—has he? He, he, he! (*laughing and chuckling*) Oh!

TONY. (*laughing and chuckling*) Ha, ha, ha!

CAPT. A. Eh?—what!—am I right? You have given me an ague!

SIR G. Have I? What do you propose doing?

CAPT. A. Dancing it off to-night at Almacks, for Lady Janet has kindly promised me her hand.

SIR G. Lady Janet, dance?

CAPT. A. To be sure—the last new Polka! I made the tour of France to be perfect in it. (*singing, and dancing*) La, la, la!

SIR G. Now that's wrong—that second step! Look here! (*gets up, but falls back again*) Oh lord!

CAPT. A. What's the matter !

SIR G. Surprised and shocked that a married woman, of her mature age, should think of such an abomination !

CAPT. A. Ah !—there she is, and I know she wishes for a rehearsal. Adieu ! and don't be so damned lazy—squatting there like a turkeyhen. La, la, la !

Exit, dancing, L.H.

SIR G. My wife dance ! inconsiderate woman !

NOISE *without of laughing and chatting.*

—What's that, Tony ?

TONY. (*looking out*) Only my lady and the Captain tee-to-tum-ing it—so. (*imitates waltzing*)

SIR G. This is pleasant—remarkably pleasant !

TONY. Well, if ever—no, never ! I declare they have got one another's arms round one another's waists ! Well, that's sociable ! Only just step this way, Sir.

SIR G. You tantalizing brute !—you know I could not stir to save my life !

TONY. Here comes my lady.

Enter LADY JANET, L.H.

LADY J. (*aside to TONY*) Is his jealousy roused ?

TONY. (*aside to her*) His head is hotter than his heels.

LADY J. (*aside to him*) Send in the children.

Exit TONY, imitating waltz.

LADY J. Dear Sir George ! and is it, then, true ? What ! and is this the dear little angry foot ? (*squeezing it with her hand*)

SIR G. Zounds, Madam, you'll pulverise me ! Yes, it is, and it belongs to a still more angry body, Lady Janet. I'm in torture !

LADY J. I know you are, darling, but (*soothingly*) 'tis only the gout.

SIR G. As you say, (*imitating*) 'tis *only* the gout !

LADY J. You see, I am calm, my dear.

SIR G. I do indeed, *my dear !*

LADY J. And I've brought all the maids to wrap you up and make you comfortable.

SIR G. That's right, Lady Janet Martyr ! Expose me to your servants—publish it to the town ! Had you not better clap a man at the corner of the street, with a board at his back ?

LADY J. Come in, girls !

Enter several MAID-SERVANTS.

SIR G. Here they are, as eager as hounds, and as ready to worry me ! And there stands my wife, as callous as an Inquisitor at an *autô-da-fè !*

Some of the SERVANTS wrap up his leg in flannel—others place pillows behind him—LADY JANET puts a flannel cap on his head.

SIR G. How delightfully agreeable! (*taking off cap*) What is this for?

LADY J. The gout may get into your head, my dear.

SIR G. (*throws cap angrily away*) Don't spare me, my dears! That's right, Lucy, crush my toes—there's a darling!

LADY J. (*to* SERVANTS) Now you may go, girls—but don't laugh.

Exeunt GIRLS, *giggling.*

SIR G. They may well laugh, when you set them an example, *my love!*

LADY J. 'Tis my duty to be cheerful, *my love!*

SIR G. And, like a good wife, your duty seems to be a pleasure, *my love!*

LADY J. Well, adieu!

SIR G. Barbarian! You are not going to leave me?

LADY J. I must away to practise for the ball to-night. Good bye! (*stopping*) How forgetful I am of my dear husband's happiness! See, dear, what a bouquet of *billets-doux* I have got for you,—there they are. I hope they'll amuse you; and if they require answers, my pen is at your service. Adieu, deary! I'll not disturb you when I come from the ball, to ask you how you are,—you can leave word with Tony. Ta-ta!

Exit L.

SIR G. Ta-ta! My astonishment has taken away the pain of my foot; for I maintain these notes are very suspicious ones, and ought to have opened any woman's eyes that are worth opening! (*smelling the notes*) A sensitive wife ought to have smelt out that something was wrong. Now, here's one with a motto, "I change but in death." That change will be mine soon. (*takes another*) "I am waiting for you,—yours, Julia." Then, Julia, you'll wait a damned long time! This pink one, here, embossed all over with little fat Cupids—signed Rosamond. "Where are you, George?" Where am I? Why, here, Ma'am, in an arm-chair, muffled up in flannel, like a muffin at Christmas! I say it was my wife's duty to have been in agonies; —I don't think hysterics would have been at all unbecoming;—and if she had taken out her scissors and stabbed me, I should have felt highly flattered by it,—it would only have been justifiable homicide. The children only came home yesterday, for the *long* vacation. A pleasant prospect I've got! But my wife! Ah! what is the pain I feel in that extremity (*pointing to his foot*) to what I feel at my other end? (*striking his forehead*) What is a diseased toe to a faithless rib? Ah! here she comes, with her capering Captain. And do they suppose my *understanding* so feeble—so—— (*tries to rise, but cannot*)

Enter LADY JANET *and* ARUNDEL, *arm-in-arm*—BELINDA *following, in feigned dejection,* L.

SIR G. Captain Arundel, if you think I will sit tamely here——

CAPT. A. Then why the deuce don't you get up?

SIR G. Do you think I can't? (*starts up and stands erect*) There!

They push away his chair.

—Sir, instead of squinting at my wife, turn to that woe-begone and deceived maiden——

BEL. (*weeps*)

SIR G. Whom you pretended to adore, only to cover a base design.

CAPT. A. Upon honour!——

SIR G. Words won't do! I say you have obtained here an improper footing!

BEL. Stand to that!

SIR G. I will, for ever! But just push the chair this way. (*he resumes his seat*)

LADY J. Fie, Sir George!

SIR G. Silence, woman! What I feel in my foot—I mean in my heart—is not to be soothed by the syren's song! I say, Sir, if you love that woe-stricken virgin, prove it!

LADY J. (*nudges* CAPTAIN ARUNDEL *and shakes her head*)

CAPT. A. (*conceitedly to* SIR GEORGE) Did you speak?

SIR G. Yes, Sir, and I repeat——

CAPT. A. Pray do, for I did not catch one syllable you uttered.

SIR G. (*with feigned composure*) Indeed!

CAPT. A. Fact, 'pon honour! (*turning, and coquetting with* LADY JANET)

SIR G. Confusion! Captain Arundel, you are no gentleman; and do me the favour to consider yourself kicked! (*aside*) for alas! I have not a kick in me!

CAPT. A. Come out, Sir, directly!

SIR G. Sir, I have my reasons for not going out.

CAPT. A. Sir George, with respect to your unworthy suspicions, I tell you, you haven't a leg to stand on; and to prove it, I should with rapture receive Belinda's hand, but cannot.

SIR G. Why not?

CAPT. A. Because her fortune——

SIR G. That subterfuge sha'n't protect you, for I here declare her fortune to be at her own disposal.

BEL. My dear Guardian! (*runs and hugs him*)

SIR G. That will do,—no raptures. (*aside to her, and winking*) Another time!

CAPT. A. ⎫
LADY J. ⎬ Ha, ha, ha! Joy—joy!
BEL. ⎭

SIR G. What! Eh? Captain—Belinda—wife! Is it a trick?

LADY J. Yes—a trick which I hope will happily finish the game, and leave us all winners;—for, with the proof of my husband's love, I can say—Dear George, come to my arms!

SIR G. And I can say—Dear Janet, your arms must come to me! Ah! (*sighs*) Could I but get rid of my gout as easily as my follies, I should be the happiest of husbands!

LADY J. Then you are the happiest, for you have no gout—a little rose-water and a change of hose will cure you.

Sir G. No gout?—no gout? (*jumps up*) Tol de rol de rol! (*skips*) Then I may dance again—but only with you, my darling Janet. Tony! Tony!—ha, ha, ha!—throw the crutches out of the window! Captain, I'll walk, ride, run, hop, swim, skate with you for a hundred! Belinda, allow me to present one who adores you.

> Tony *advances modestly behind*—Sir George *joins the hands of* Belinda *and* Arundel.

Tony. Oh!
Sir G. But what caused these cursed twinges?
Bel. Oh, Tony must explain that.
Sir G. Tony!

> They turn and see him extended in a chair.

—Tony!
Tony. Coming!
Bel. What's the matter, Tony?
Tony. Ah! that voice!
Bel. Are you dying, Tony?
Tony. In course I am!
Brl. Give him air.
Tony. I want no air—I want spirits! (*starting up*) But I'll be revenged! I'll give you all——
Bel. What? Poison?
Tony. No—warning!

> *Rushes off* L.H.

Sir G. I confess I have been playing the fool; but as it is not the first time I have done so (*to the* Audience) and have been forgiven, I trust, with your permission, it will not be the last;—and if I am the first of the *Martyrs* who ever solicited a repetition of his " First Fit of the Gout," it is in the hope that I shall find a sovereign remedy in your indulgent approbation.

Captain A.   Belinda.   Sir George.   Jady Janet.

R.   L.

Curtain.

LACY'S ACTING EDITION—New Plays, 6d. eac